MEET THE GIRL TALK CHARACTERS

Sabrina Wells is petite, with curly auburn hair, sparkling hazel eyes, and a bubbly personality. Sabrina loves magazines, shopping, sleepovers, and most of all, she loves talking to her best friends.

Katie Campbell is a straight-A student and super athlete. With her blond hair, blue eyes, and matching clothes, she's everyone's idea of little miss perfect. But Katie has a few surprises for everyone, including herself!

Randy Zak has just moved to Acorn Falls from New York City, and is she ever cool! With her 'radical' spiked haircut and her hip New York clothes, Randy teaches everyone just how much fun it is to be different.

Allison Cloud is a Native American Indian. Allison's super smart and really beautiful. But she has one major problem: She's thirteen years old, five foot seven, and still growing!

Here's what they're talking about in
Girl Talk

RANDY: Al, our class ski trip is going to be awesome!

ALLISON: I know, I'm excited about it, too. All that snow and trees; it's going to be great.

RANDY: I can't believe we have to share a cabin with Stacy the Great and her clones.

ALLISON: Yeah, I know what you mean. But listen, something is bothering me even more than that.

RANDY: What?

ALLISON: Well, suppose Eagle Mountain is haunted?

THE GHOST OF EAGLE MOUNTAIN

By L.E. Blair

GIRL TALK® series created by Western Publishing Company, Inc.

Produced by Angel Entertainment, Inc.

Western Publishing Company, Inc., Racine, Wisconsin 53404

Text by B.B. Calhoun

Chapter One

"I found us! I found us!" Katie called from the front of the crowd around the seventh-grade bulletin board. She waved her arms excitedly to get our attention.

"Where?" Sabrina asked quickly, standing on her toes to look over the shoulders of the people in front of her. "I can't see."

"It's the fifth column from the left," I told her, pointing it out. My name's Allison Cloud. I was standing with my best friends Sabrina, Randy, and Katie, and almost every other seventh grader at Bradley Junior High trying to read a list of names on the class bulletin board, trying to find their names.

Sabs continued to complain. "All I can see is the heading at the top: 'Cabin Assignments.'"

Sabs pushed her curly auburn hair behind her ears and looked up at me. "I wish I was as

1

tall as you are, Allison."

"No, you don't," I assured her. Being tall isn't always fun. I should know — I'm five feet seven inches tall and still growing. If I had a choice, I'd rather be four feet ten and three-quarter inches tall, like Sabrina.

"They put all of us in the same cabin!" Katie announced, pushing her way back through the crowd to us. As usual, Katie looked terrific. Her honey blond hair was pulled back into a ponytail and tied with aice blue ribbon. She wore a long-sleeved, ice-blue-and-white striped polo shirt and matching ice blue pants. Today she had on white moccasins with little blue and white balls hanging on them.

"Ahh right! This is going to be the absolute best part of the whole year," Sabrina began dramatically. "Three days on a snow-covered mountain..."

"Hey, Al, Katie, Sabs! Wait up a second," a familiar voice called from behind us. I turned around and saw Randy Zak elbowing her way past the group at the bulletin board. Randy, Katie, Sabrina, and I are best friends, and we do everything together.

"Hi, Randy. Great outfit," said Sabrina. Randy used to live in New York, and her clothes are a bit unusual compared to what everybody wears in Acorn Falls, Minnesota. Today she was wearing a white hat, a black mock turtleneck that went down to her knees, white stretch pants, black socks, and white sneakers with black tic-tac-toe boards painted on them. A red X dangled from one ear, and a red O from the other.

"Can you believe the cabin assignment list for this weekend?" Randy asked, frowning and pushing her hat farther back on her head.

"Isn't it great? We all got into the same cabin!" Katie answered with a smile, her blond ponytail bobbing from side to side as she nodded.

"Great," Randy grumbled as we headed down the hall toward the seventh-grade lockers. "Except for. . ."

Before she could even finish her sentence, Stacy Hansen's piercing voice cut in from across the hall.

"Don't look now, girls, but it's the cabin crashers," Stacy said to her ever-present clones, Eva Malone, Laurel Spencer, and B.Z.

Latimer. Stacy's father, Mr. Hansen, is the principal of Bradley Junior High, so Stacy always acts as if she's better than the rest of us. She's so stuck up that we call her Stacy the Great.

"I can't believe we have to share a cabin with them!" Laurel exclaimed, rolling her eyes.

"If I wasn't just dying to use my brand-new cross-country skis," Stacy continued, flipping her wavy blond hair back over her shoulder, "I don't think I'd even go on this trip."

"This is awful!" Eva complained loudly. "I mean, talk about rotten luck!"

"I'll bet they all snore, too," B.Z. snickered.

"Come on, girls," Stacy the Great commanded. "Let's go find Nick and the other boys and find out which cabin they're in."

"What were they talking about?" Sabrina asked.

"That's what I was trying to tell you," Randy answered sourly. "Remember what Mr. Hansen told us about those cabins? Each one has a little room for a chaperon and just enough bunks for —"

"Eight people," I remembered suddenly.

"Oh, no!" Sabrina wailed, hiding her face in her hands.

4

"You mean —" Katie began, her eyes wide as she stared at Randy.

"Yeah." Randy nodded. "They put the four of us together, all right. Together with Stacy the Great and her clones!"

"This has got to be the worst thing that's ever happened to us!" Sabrina moaned. "The whole trip is going to be ruined!"

"Too bad they didn't ask us to list the people that we didn't want to stay with as well as the people we did," Randy said, sighing. I knew just how she felt. Matter of fact, I don't think any of us was looking forward to sharing a cabin with Stacy the Great.

Just then the warning bell rang. It meant that there were only five minutes left before class started, and none of us had been to our lockers yet. Randy's locker is right across the hall from mine, so we went together.

"What a major-league pain," Randy said as we walked. "That bingo-head Stacy is going to ruin the whole trip."

"I don't know," I told her. "If we try and stay out of their way —"

"How are we going to do that?" Randy asked. "Cabin fifty-three is not going to be all that big, you know." Suddenly a shiver ran through me "Which cabin did you say we were going to be in?" I asked her.

"Cabin fifty-three," Randy repeated. For some reason, hearing the number of our cabin twisted my stomach into knots.

When we reached our lockers, I fumbled with my lock, trying to calm myself down. What was wrong with me? Why did our cabin number bother me?

As I opened the door of my locker, something fell from the top shelf and floated to the floor at my feet. Absently, I bent down and picked it up. It was something very soft and wide in my hand. It was a feather. How had a feather got into my locker? I hadn't put it there. And I didn't have a locker partner.

I took another look at the feather and suddenly realized that I knew just what kind of bird it had come from. It was an eagle feather, just like the ones my grandfather's father had handed down to him before he died on the reservation.

"Hey, Al," Randy's called. "See you in homeroom!"

I put the feather back on the shelf, grabbed

my books for first period, and closed the locker. Giving myself a shake, I hurried down the hall toward math class.

By the time I joined Sabrina, Randy, and Katie at lunch, I had forgotten about the feather and the strange feeling I'd had when I heard our cabin assignment. I was starting to look forward to the ski trip again, in spite of our unwelcome cabin mates. I could tell that Sabrina, Randy, and Katie were feeling better about it, too.

"Who cares about Stacy the Great," Randy said, spooning up some macaroni and cheese. "I've never been skiing before, and I think this is going to be an awesome trip. I can just see myself now, cruising down the slopes —"

"Randy," Katie said, giggling. "This is a cross-country ski trip. You don't cruise down the slopes on cross-country skis. You follow trails through the woods and stuff."

"Oh. But I thought we were going to Eagle Mountain," Randy responded.

"We are," Sabrina told her, picking up an apple from her tray of fruit. "But we don't have any real mountains in Minnesota. Eagle Mountain is just a big hill."

"Is cross-country skiing hard?" Randy asked Katie. Katie is the best athlete of all of us. She's even on the boys' ice-hockey team.

"I've only gone a couple of times," Katie explained. "I thought it was really fun, though, and I can't wait to try it again."

"Maybe I'll just hang around inside all day," Sabs said doubtfully. "I'm not sure I want to ski all day. Sitting in front of a fire just seems so much nicer."

"Don't worry," Katie said encouragingly. "I think you'll enjoy it."

"Unless you get lost in the woods," Randy teased.

"Lost on Eagle Mountain," I mumbled, feeling my stomach tighten. "That doesn't sound like much fun to me." Randy looked over at me quickly, frowning. I turned back to Sabrina before Randy could ask what was bothering me.

"I don't think I'll get lost —" Sabrina's eyes suddenly got very wide and her face turned bright red. "There he is!" she gasped.

"There *who* is?" Randy asked, swiveling around to see what Sabs was staring at.

"It's Greg Loggins," Sabrina sighed. "Isn't

he gorgeous?"

Greg Loggins was Sabrina's latest crush. He was new at Bradley, so we didn't really know him yet. But he had started hanging around with Sabrina's twin brother, Sam. Sabrina thought he was just perfect.

"Is he coming this way?" Sabrina asked, trying to hide her face by staring at her lunch tray. "No! Don't look!"

"But you just told us to find out if he was coming this way," Katie said, laughing.

"Al, you look," Sabrina begged. "If only one of us looks, then it won't be so obvious."

I turned around as casually as I could. Greg was standing in the middle of the cafeteria, looking for a place to sit. After a moment, he noticed an empty spot at our table and began to walk toward us.

"Hi," he said when he reached the table. He shook a lock of his straight blond hair out of his eyes. "Listen, is anyone sitting —"

At that moment there was a shout from a table across the room. "Greg! Over here! We saved you a seat!"

It was Sabrina's brother Sam, who was sitting with his friends Nick and Jason. Greg turned his head and waved.

"Be right there," Greg called back. Without another look at our table, he walked across to where his friends were sitting.

"Boy!" Sabrina exclaimed. "One of these days I'm really going to let Sam have it. He always manages to mess up my life."

I was sure that Sam hadn't done it on purpose, but I knew that Sabrina didn't want to listen to that.

"Think of it this way, Sabs," Katie said cheerfully. "Greg would have sat here if Sam hadn't called him. That means that he must have wanted to sit at this table, at least a little bit."

"Yeah, I guess so," Sabrina said, brightening. "I guess that's a 'Yes' signal. *Young Chic* says that you should look for signals that a boy sends out. There are 'Yes' signals and 'No' signals. I think I'll keep track of both."

Randy looked at me, smiled, and rolled her eyes. The bell suddenly rang, and we all rushed off to our classes. It was hard to concentrate in class, since all everybody could think about and talk about was the ski trip. Still, it was one of the longest weeks, I could ever remember. It was weird to be excited about something and kind of dreading it at the same time. I also couldn't stop wondering about that eagle feather and where it had come from. But finally, Thursday night came. We were leaving for Eagle Mountain in the morning.

Chapter Two

After school on Thursday, I ran straight home, pulled my duffel bag out from under my bed, and started looking through my drawers and closets for the warmest clothes I could find. By six o'clock, all I had packed were two books, my sleeping bag, and a pillow. I was too excited to think.

"What do you think I should pack for the trip?" I asked my mother when we sat down to dinner.

"Where are you going, Allison?" my little brother, Charlie, asked. "Can I go too?"

"I'm going skiing with my class, to Eagle Mountain," I explained to Charlie.

My grandmother, Nooma, made a funny noise almost like a whimper. I turned to ask her what was wrong, but she just stood up and started carrying her dishes into the kitchen.

"Evil Mountain!" Charlie exclaimed. "That sounds scary. I want to go."

"It's *Eagle* Mountain," my mother correct-
ed. "It's not scary."

"Evil Mountain. Evil Mountain," Charlie
was saying. "I want to go to Evil Mountain
with Allison."

"Eagle Mountain," my mom repeated.
"And Allison is going on a cross-country skiing trip with the seventh grade. When you are
in seventh grade, you can go."

I followed Nooma into the kitchen. She was
sitting at the kitchen counter, staring out the
window. I put my plates down by the sink and
sat down next to her.

"Nooma?" I said quietly.

She looked up. All of a sudden she looked
very tired — and old.

"Why did you make that funny noise when
I mentioned Eagle Mountain?" I asked her.

Nooma sighed and looked out the window
again. "Well, Eagle Mountain has an old story,"
she began. "It's from the time when the white
settlers first came here. Our people lived in
areas stretching from here, around the Great
Lakes, all the way into what is now Canada."

I thought about that for a minute. I had
learned a little from my grandparents about

the history of our people, the Chippewa, and how, after the settlers came, they had been moved to a couple of different reservations in the state of Minnesota. My grandparents and even my parents had grown up on reservations, but my parents had both gone away to boarding school. After college, they got married and decided to live in Acorn Falls. About five years ago, Nooma and Grandpa moved in with us.

Anyway, my grandparents taught me that when the settlers came, the Chippewa had been forced to give almost all the land in the area to the American government. I had never really thought about how much land that had been.

My grandmother went on with her story, and I listened carefully. "There was a large group of Chippewa living at the base of the hills where you are going," she explained. "The chief of this tribe was a man named Eagle Feather. His wife was named Running Deer. She was very kind and good and beautiful. Eagle Feather and Running Deer loved each other from their childhood, and they hated to be apart. Their happiness when they were together was so great that you could see it just by looking at them."

In my mind, I could picture the strong, handsome Chippewa chief and his beautiful wife looking lovingly into each other's eyes.

"A year after their marriage, the chief and his wife had a baby. He was healthy and strong. They named him Little Wolf. When the settlers came to Minnesota, Eagle Feather was determined to protect the land and the hills for his people, especially for the wife and son he loved so much."

"What happened?" I asked eagerly.

"One evening, as the sun was setting, Running Deer put Little Wolf to sleep, singing the lullaby she sang to him every night. At that moment, the word came — there was to be a great battle against the settlers. Eagle Feather went to fight, leaving Running Deer and Little Wolf behind.

"Eagle Feather and his tribe fought bravely, but in the end they were forced to flee. They managed to escape through the woods up into the hills. There was no moon that night, so Eagle Feather sneaked back through the darkness to save his wife and son. But when he got to their home, they had vanished."

My grandmother looked at me, and I felt that shiver run up and down my spine again.

"Eagle Feather went back into the hills," she continued, "to what is now called Eagle Mountain. After that, he was only seen at night, walking through the woods, singing the lullaby that Running Deer sang to Little Wolf. Eagle Feather roamed the hills, looking for his beloved wife and son. After fifty-three days, Eagle Feather, too, disappeared. Some say he lost his mind from sorrow. Some say he died from cold. But some say he roams the mountain still."

I swallowed hard, and for a moment I couldn't speak. "But, Nooma," I said finally, "that was almost two hundred years ago, wasn't it? I mean, no one thinks that Eagle Feather is still alive, do they?"

"No one knows what became of him after the fifty-three days. It is said that the spirit of Eagle Feather cannot be at peace until he finds the spirit of his love, Running Deer."

I thought for a moment. "So you are afraid for me to spend the night on Eagle Mountain?" I asked.

She nodded. "The spirit of Eagle Feather is made angry if he is not left alone on the mountain to look for his family."

"Nooma," I said slowly, "what was the song that Running Deer sang to Little Wolf?"

My grandmother started to sing. She repeated different Chippewa words over and over to a beautiful melody. After a few measures she stopped.

"You know it?" she asked.

"Of course," I said in a hushed voice. I could feel my heart beating faster.

"The song has been with our people for many generations. My mother sang it to me, and I sang it to your father when he was a baby. I sang it to you and Charlie, too."

"Would you sing it again, please?" I asked.

Nooma closed her eyes and began to sing again. Her voice was kind of crackly, but the song was still comforting. It was so familiar, even though I hadn't heard it in years. I looked at the doorway, and my mother was standing there watching Nooma, a peaceful smile on her face. When my grandmother saw her, she stopped singing, stood up, and walked over to the sink to start the dishes.

"I can finish the lullaby," said my mother.

"Will you teach me?" I asked.

My mother sat down and began to sing, softly at first, and then louder.

"Otter, go to your home by the river, and Deer,
to lie in the woods.
Wolf, run back to your den, and Eagle, fly
to your perch.
Rabbit, crawl into your hole, and Serpent,
slide into your nest.
Wildcat, lay your head on your paws, and Bear,
crawl into your cave.
Owl and Moon, watch over them all. . ."

Nooma joined my mother and sang the last line with her, very softly.

". . .and Child, close your eyes and sleep with
the world."

I closed my eyes. I could remember being a baby and falling asleep listening to that song.

When I opened my eyes, my grandmother was busy washing dishes again, and my mother had started folding laundry. I left the kitchen and went up to my bedroom to do my homework and finish packing. I kept thinking about Eagle Feather, Running Deer, and Little Wolf.

I have never really believed in ghosts and spirits, but there was something about this story that almost felt real. Somehow Eagle Feather's story seemed more real to me than just a part of history or an old ghost story.

Chapter Three

Sabrina calls Allison:

ALLISON: Hello. Allison Cloud speaking.

SABRINA: Al, it's Sabrina. And you are not going to believe this!

ALLISON: What is it? Is something wrong?

SABRINA: No. Nothing's wrong. Listen! Guess what my brother Sam just happened to mention to me tonight, as if it was totally unimportant!

ALLISON: Does it have something to do with Greg Loggins?

SABRINA: (*amazed*) Allison! How did you know?

ALLISON: It was just a guess.

SABRINA: Anyway, Sam just told me that he and Nick and Jason and Greg Loggins are all going to be in the same cabin this weekend! And

	guess which cabin they're in!
ALLISON:	Which one?
SABRINA:	Cabin fifty-four! Since we're in cabin fifty-three, that means they'll be right next door!
ALLISON:	That's great, Sabs. Now you'll really have a chance to get to know Greg.
SABRINA:	I know. I can hardly wait! But now I'll never be able to decide what to bring. I think I'll call Randy and ask her — she's awesome with clothes. Talk to you later, Al.
ALLISON:	Bye Sabrina.

Katie calls Allison:

CHARLIE:	Bang! Bang!
ALLISON:	Charlie, give me the phone!

(*There is a scuffle. Charlie is making machine-gun noises.*)

ALLISON:	Charlie! Let go of the phone! Hello?
KATIE:	Hi, Allison. It's Katie.
ALLISON:	Hi. Sorry about Charlie.

KATIE: It's okay. I think he's cute. Anyway, I just called to ask you about our homework for English.

ALLISON: Katie, I don't believe this! Even I can't think about homework tonight.

KATIE: Neither can I, that's my problem. (*Katie laughs.*) Do you think you could help me with it sometime this weekend?

ALLISON: Sure! No problem. Just bring the book with you, and we'll work on it when we have time.

KATIE: Thanks! I've got to get back to packing now.

ALLISON: Me ,too. See you tomorrow.

KATIE: Bye!

Allison calls Randy:

RANDY: Yo! Randy here!

ALLISON: (*laughing*) Hello, Randy. It's Allison.

RANDY: Al! I'm glad you called. Listen. What kind of music system do you think they'll have in the cab-

	ins? Should I bring my tapes or my CDs?
ALLISON:	Randy, I don't think they're going to have a music system up there.
RANDY:	(*shocked*) They aren't?
ALLISON:	No, I don't think so.
RANDY:	Al, I have to go. I've got to pack my Walkman and a whole bunch of tapes. I can't make it through the weekend without music! *Ciao!*
ALLISON:	(quietly) Hey, Randy. Something strange happened today.
RANDY:	What?
ALLISON:	I found a eagle feather in my locker at school.
RANDY:	A what? How weird! How do you know it's an eagle feather?
ALLISON:	My grandfather has a whole collection of them because the birds are so rare. But he keeps the feathers in a case.
RANDY:	Well, one of the feathers must have fallen out of the case and caught on your clothes or something.

ALLISON: I'm sure that must be it, but I haven't been anywhere near grandfather's collection.

RANDY: Don't worry about it, Al. What ever the reason, it's got to be a logical reason, right?

ALLISON: Right! See you tommorrow, Randy.

RANDY: Ciao!

Chapter Four

Thursday night I had a strange dream. I was walking through the woods in summer. For some reason, I was happy and excited. I felt like singing, but at the same time I knew that I was supposed to be very quiet. I walked on for a little while until I came to a familiar place. I knew there was going to be a little clearing just ahead.

I took another few steps forward and found myself blinking at the bright sunlight in the small, hidden clearing. In the middle of the clearing stood a tall, dark man with deep brown eyes and black hair. He was smiling at me gently, and the sight of him made my heart leap. In his arms he was holding a small bundle wrapped in a blanket.

I stood still. The man in the clearing walked toward me and offered me the bundle. Carefully, I reached out and took it from him. I pulled a corner of the blanket away and looked down into the sleeping face of a very young baby.

"We will call him Little Wolf," the man said quietly. "And he will grow up to be proud and free, my Running Deer." Then the sun faded and I fell back into a sleep without dreams.

When the alarm went off on Friday morning, I had a major case of what my mother calls "the butterflies" in my stomach. It was the day of the ski trip. I looked at the clock and quickly jumped out of bed. I put on an old pair of jeans, a long underwear top, and a heavy gold sweater that used to be my dad's. It's my absolute favorite sweater, and I always feel better when I wear it.

It took me so long to get ready, I didn't have time for breakfast. That was okay with me, though. I didn't have much of an appetite anyway.

I brought my bag into the front hall, where my father was waiting. He had offered to drive me to school on his way to work. It's kind of difficult to ride a bicycle with a duffel bag. My mom came running downstairs to give me a hug and a kiss, and I could see those little wrinkles that come out in her forehead whenever she's concerned.

"Don't worry, Mom, it's only three days," I told her, but we both knew that she would worry anyway.

On my way out the door, my grandmother scurried up behind me and handed me a paper bag filled with corn cakes she had made for me. She's always making stuff like that and trying to get me to take it with me when I leave the house. It's as though she thinks I'm going out into the wilderness and she's afraid I'm going to starve or something.

I told her that the bus ride was only a couple of hours long and that we'd be there before lunch.

"You never know," she said, pushing the bag into my arms. "No one can know what the world has waiting for them. You must always be prepared for what may happen."

I could tell she wasn't going to take no for an answer, so I thanked her and stuffed the bag into my knapsack.

When we pulled into the school parking lot, there were bunches of kids hanging around near the buses with their knapsacks and duffel bags. There were a few parents hanging around, too, embarrassing their kids by saying good-bye for too long. I was thankful when my father didn't get out of the car, but turned instead to look at me from his seat.

"Allison —" he began, as if he were going to say something very serious.

I looked at him, waiting for him to continue. But all he said was "I want you to really enjoy yourself." I could tell that there was something he wasn't saying, but I didn't know how to ask what it was.

So I just nodded and hugged him good-bye.

"Really, Al," he repeated as I got out of the car and pulled my duffel bag and knapsack out from the backseat. "Have a wonderful time."

"Thanks, Daddy," I said, and closed the car door. I slowly walked across the parking lot toward the buses. Then I turned around and waved to my father. After that I started walking more quickly, because I really wanted to find Randy, Sabs, and Katie. I passed a huge crowd of seventh graders talking and laughing with their friends. Everyone was so excited, I couldn't help getting a bit more excited myself

— especially when I spotted Randy and Katie, who broke into huge smiles when they saw me.

"Get over here, Al!" Katie yelled.

"We're on our way!" Randy screamed out. I don't think I'd ever seen her more excited. It definitely rubbed off on me. I started thinking of the hills and the woods and snowball fights and hanging out with my friends, and I thought, *Sabs could be right! This could end up being the highlight of seventh grade!*

"Hey, where's Sabs?" I asked, realizing that I hadn't seen her. Of course, I wasn't too surprised to learn that she hadn't arrived yet. Sometimes it takes Sabs a little extra time to get ready for a big event.

Just then we heard a loud voice from near one of the buses. It was Stacy.

"Be careful with those!" she was yelling at the bus driver as he loaded her skis into the luggage compartment near the bottom of the bus.

"Stacy's probably the only person in the whole seventh grade who brought her own cross-country skis instead of renting from the lodge," said Katie.

"Yeah, figures," muttered Randy. "Let's definitely not get on that bus."

"I'll tell you one thing," I said, looking around at the buses, which were quickly filling up. "If we don't want to ride on that bus, we'd better find another one that still has room on it, or we won't even be able to sit together."

"But what about Sabrina?" said Katie.

Randy looked around. "Al's right," she said. "We have to get into action now."

"We'll save Sabrina a seat," I promised.

We picked up our gear and started to walk toward the only bus that looked like it had any room left.

Just then Sabrina came rushing up behind us, dragging two huge duffel bags behind her. She was breathing hard, and her face was pretty red.

"Sabrina, what happened?" I asked her.

"What took you so long?" said Katie.

Sabrina took a deep breath. "Oh, I just couldn't decide what to bring," she told us.

Randy laughed. "Well, it looks like you decided to bring everything!"

"Well," Sabs said quietly. "I know you're not used to such cold weather. So I brought a few extra sweaters. It's cold up on a mountain. You need to bring a lot of clothes."

Randy gave her a big smile. "Thanks, Sabs. You're the best."

"Come on, you guys," I said, leading the way over to the last bus. "Let's go."

We watched as our bags were loaded onto the bus, and then we climbed on board, finding ourselves face-to-face with Miss Miller, our science teacher. She was sitting in the front row, next to Mr. Byrne, who teaches shop. Miss Miller was wearing this long wool coat that was about three sizes too big for her. Worst of all, it was red plaid with yellow, green, and blue stripes in it. And she even had a matching hat! Mr. Byrne had his head buried in a book. He looked pretty funny with his big beard and his earmuffs. Miss Miller smiled when she saw us.

"Oh, good," she said "My girls! Or half of them, that is. I guess we'll be rooming together for the next few days."

"Hi, Miss Miller," I said.

"Are you the teacher for our cabin?" Sabrina asked.

"That's right," said Miss Miller cheerfully.

"Have you seen our other four cabin mates around?"

"We sure have," said Randy, rolling her eyes.

"I'm pretty sure they got on one of the other buses," said Katie, trying not to giggle.

"Well, then, I guess we'll meet up with them there," said Miss Miller. She reached into the duffel bag at her feet, pulled out a bright blue plaid scarf, and wrapped it around her neck. Randy looked like she was going to be sick. She mumbled something about being allergic to plaid and ran toward the back of the bus.

Luckily, we managed to find four seats together. In a few moments, the bus was full. Everyone was talking and laughing, and one boy had turned on a radio, so it was really noisy. Even Miss Miller and Mr. Byrne kept twisting around in their seats. I could hardly wait for the bus to start moving so that we could get to Eagle Mountain.

Finally, the bus driver, a short, round man, got on. He introduced himself as Gus. Gus reminded me of an elf. He fiddled around for a few minutes and then started the engine. A cheer went up from the bus. We were off!

It seemed as if we had hardly left Acorn Falls when Gus turned on the loudspeaker system.

"Okeydokey," he called out, "it's time to start some singing! Will the young man with the radio kindly turn it off?"

We looked at each other in surprise. It wasn't that it was unusual for kids to sing on a bus ride. After all, it had happened on almost every field trip I had ever been on. But usually the bus driver tried to get the kids to keep quiet. I had certainly never heard of a bus driver *telling* kids to sing on the bus. This Gus was turning out to be a pretty unusual character.

"Come on," he went on, "doesn't anybody know 'Found A Peanut'? Here we go:

Found a peanut,
Found a peanut,
Found a peanut, last night,
Last night I found a peanut,
Found a peanut, last night!"

Everybody started laughing. Then a couple of kids joined in, and soon the whole bus was singing together. I couldn't help wondering what grumpy old Mr. Byrne up in the front of the bus thought of all this.

A little while later, after we had gotten through "Row, Row, Row Your Boat," and "On Top of Spaghetti," and were in the middle of "The Bear Went Over the Mountain," the bus suddenly started jerking and making loud noises. My stomach started doing flip-flops.

"What's that?" someone asked.

"What's happening?"

"What's wrong?"

"Nothing at all to worry about," said Gus. He pulled the bus over to the side of the road. After a couple of loud bangs, the engine stopped completely.

Miss Miller stood up and turned around to face us, adjusting her red plaid hat every few seconds. "Everybody just stay in your seats, please," she said as Gus got out of the bus. "I'm sure that Mr. . . .uh. . .Gus will be able to fix the problem shortly."

"Oh, no. I hope this doesn't mean we're stuck here," Katie said.

"Are we going to miss the ski trip?" I heard someone ask.

Gus climbed back into the bus. "Well, it looks like we might be here for a little while," he announced. "We got ourselves a little problem. Could be the alternator. I'll radio in for another bus, but it'll be at least an hour before they can get it up here."

No one really felt like singing anymore, so we sat quietly waiting for the other bus to come rescue us. I began to feel a bit nervous again. We hadn't even reached Eagle Mountain, but we had already had lots of bad luck. First, Stacy the Great and her friends were assigned as our cabin mates. Now our bus had broken down. What was next?

Katie and Sabs were talking quietly across the aisle, and Randy had pulled out her Walkman, so I decided to read for awhile. I was rereading The Chronicles of Narnia by C. S. Lewis, which is one of my favorite series. It's all about these four children who become kings and queens in this magical land called Narnia. It always makes me feel happy and safe to read those books, which is why I brought them with me.

Since the engine was off and there was no heat in the bus, it started to get pretty cold.

"Brrrrr, it's freezing in here," said Randy, rubbing her hands together.

"Really," Sabrina agreed. "I wish I could get to all those sweaters I packed, but they're in my duffel bag under the bus."

I began to feel a rumbling in my stomach. I wished I had eaten some breakfast.

It was as if Katie had read my mind. "I'm getting really hungry," she said.

"Me too," said Randy.

"I wonder how long we're going to be here," said Sabrina. "I'd give anything for a bag of potato chips."

Suddenly, I remembered the corn cakes my grandmother had packed for me. They weren't exactly potato chips, but they were food. I guess maybe she knew what she was talking about when she said that no one can know what's waiting for them and that you should always be prepared for whatever might happen.

I opened my knapsack and pulled out the paper bag.

"I have something we can eat," I said, pulling out four corn cakes, each wrapped in aluminum foil.

"What are they?" asked Katie.

"They're corn cakes. My grandmother

made them."

Randy bit into hers. "Wow, Al, they're delicious!"

Sabrina nodded in agreement, her mouth full.

Suddenly, we heard a cheer from the back of the bus. The new bus had arrived! We quickly swallowed the rest of our corn cakes and gathered up our things.

It felt much better to be in the warm new bus, with our stomachs full of corn cakes. Gus even started everybody singing again. I didn't notice the time passing, but suddenly, we were there.

The bus pulled up in front of a big wooden lodge with two huge smoking chimneys. The ground was covered with clean white snow, except where someone had cleared paths through the trees. The trees were mostly evergreens, tall and covered with snow. It was really beautiful and really cold. My breath came out like little white clouds.

Meanwhile, Gus had unloaded the duffel bags from the bottom of the bus. Randy, Katie, Sabs, and I found ours in the pile. We walked toward the lodge with the other kids from our bus, waving good-bye to Gus.

"See you Sunday!" he called.

We were met at the door of the lodge by two smiling people in identical dark blue parkas, blue ski pants, knitted white hats with little blue pom-poms on top, and blue-and-white moon boots. They even had the same blond hair, with bangs cut straight across the front. At first I wasn't sure if they were two men or two women.

"Ah, the last bus! We're glad you made it!" they called out in unison as we approached.

"I'm Ranger Rhonda," the first one said cheerfully. When she smiled, you could see all of her teeth. They were very white.

"And I'm Ranger Rob," the second one announced. His smile was the same as Ranger Rhonda's. I noticed that he was about an inch taller, but that was the only difference between the two of them that I could see.

"Welcome to Eagle Mountain," they said together.

"Are they for real?" Randy whispered to me, staring at the rangers as they went to greet Miss Miller and Mr. Byrne.

I looked at Sabrina and Katie. They looked

like they were about to burst out laughing any second.

Just then something big and gray ran out of the woods and straight toward me. It looked like a wolf! I opened my mouth to scream, but I couldn't make a sound. Suddenly, it jumped on me and knocked me on my back in the snow. Its mouth started coming closer to mine. I started to panic and push it away. The next thing I knew, a warm tongue was licking my face and long white whiskers were tickling my cheek.

"Alfie!" Ranger Rhonda yelled, running over. "Alfie, get off!"

"Is he a dog?" Katie asked, pushing the furry snout away from my face and helping me stand up. Everyone else was laughing. "It looks so much like a wolf."

"That's Alfie, the camp dog," Ranger Rob explained. "He's a mutt, but we think he may actually be part wolf."

I was still trying to catch my breath and calm down, so I just watched while Sabs, Randy, and Katie petted Alfie. Just then Miss Miller walked over to where we were standing. I noticed that the suitcase she was carrying was mainly black, with gray-and- white stripes and boxes to make it plaid. Randy pointed to it and rolled her eyes.

"You girls go on ahead to the cabin," Miss Miller said. "I imagine the other four are already there. I have some things to discuss with Ranger Rhonda."

"Oh, sure," said Ranger Rhonda cheerfully. "You'll want to get settled in. The cabins are all right down that path. You can't miss yours; they're all numbered."

We set out down the path to find our cabin, dragging our duffel bags behind us in the snow. There it was, number fifty-three. All of a sudden I felt that familiar shiver run down my spine. It was really weird. I shook myself gently and followed the others up the steps. My dad would have said that I'd been reading too many scary stories, but I knew it wasn't that. I really felt strange.

"Well, here we are," Sabrina said, pushing open the door of the cabin. She bumped straight into B.Z. Latimer, who was on her way out. Behind her was something that looked like a big pink Easter bunny, but turned out to be Stacy the Great wearing a pink ski jumpsuit, pink mittens, a pink hat with a pink pom-pom, and pink moon boots.

"Oh," said Stacy, rolling her eyes, "it's our cabin mates!"

"What took you so long?" B.Z. snickered. "Did you stop to look at the scenery?"

Stacy pushed past us. "Come on, let's go," she said to B.Z. "Eva and Laurel are waiting for us."

We walked into the cabin. It was pretty bare, but clean. The walls were wood and had lots of initials carved into them. Two sides of the room were lined with bunk beds. There was one door at the back labeled 'Bathroom', and another one that led to the chaperon's room. It didn't look very big. I couldn't help wondering how Miss Miller and her plaid coat were going to fit.

As Katie, Randy, Sabs, and I looked around the room, it didn't take us long to see that the bunks on the right side were in much better shape than the ones on the left. Two of the bunks on the left were sagging, and one of the beds was being held together by rope. There was even a little hole in one of the mattresses, and the stuffing was starting to come out. But the thing I noticed was that Stacy, Eva, Laurel, and B.Z. had already spread out their sleeping bags on the four good bunks on the right.

Sabrina dropped her two duffel bags in the middle of the floor. "I can't believe those guys took all the best beds!" she said.

Somehow, I could believe it. First the bus breaks down, and now this. Luck just didn't seem to be with us on this trip.

Chapter Five

"Girls! You're still here?" Miss Miller gasped as she entered the cabin, dragging her suitcase behind her. "If you don't get up to the lodge now, you'll miss lunch. Afternoon activities are scheduled to start in about twenty minutes. I think you all have ski lessons!"

"Excellent!" Randy exclaimed, pulling on an extra sweater. "I could use a few pointers on my technique."

"What technique?" Sabs asked. "I thought you had never been on skis before."

"I haven't," Randy answered. "That's why I may need one or two small pointers."

Sometimes I envy Randy. She's always so confident in new situations. We were walking back down the path to the lodge when all of a sudden I heard someone yell, "ATTACK!" I saw Sam and his friends Nick, Jason, and Greg running toward us with snowballs in their hands.

"Stop it, you guys!" Sabrina shrieked, but the boys just kept on coming. Poor Sabs was getting pelted from all sides. Greg seemed to be aiming for her face — and he was right on target every time. But Sabs didn't let him get away with it. She has a wicked fastball, and she hit Greg in the face just as often. Randy, Katie, and I put up a pretty good fight, too, until Mr. Byrne walked by and blew his whistle.

"Is this where you people are supposed to be?" he asked gruffly.

"We're on our way, sir," Nick answered, saluting.

The four of us ran ahead of Sam and his friends and joined the lunch line. Each of us grabbed juice, a sandwich, and some fruit, then sat down at one of the tables near the fireplace.

"I'm going to kill Sam!" Sabs exclaimed as she tried to brush the snow from her hat, jacket, and sweater.

"Seems to me that Greg's the one you should be mad at," Randy said. "He's the one who kept aiming at your face!"

"Unless that's just his way of paying attention to you," Katie suggested, trying to calm Sabrina down.

"You think so?" Sabs asked, looking excited.

"You never know," Katie said. I knew Katie was just trying to help, but I didn't know why she bothered. Sabrina thought Greg was really cute, but something told me that he wasn't as nice a guy as she thought.

I looked around the lodge and noticed that it was almost empty.

"Don't you think we should figure out where we're supposed to be?" I asked.

"Let's check the activities board," Katie suggested.

We walked over and looked at the sheets of paper tacked up on the board. I found my name listed in a group for beginning ski lessons. Randy and Sabs were also in my group, but Katie had been assigned to the intermediate section.

There was a huge room at the back of the lodge where we went to rent our skis. Ranger Rhonda and some of her assistants were there to help fit us.

"How tall are you?" she asked when it was my turn.

"Five foot seven," I told her.

"Try these," she said, handing me the longest pair of skis I'd ever seen. Cross-country skis are really thin, and I couldn't imagine how I would be able to stand on them.

"Are you sure they're not too long?" I asked.

"They'll be perfect," she said. I wasn't so sure. But at least I didn't have any trouble finding boots. I knew there had to be something good about wearing a size eight and a half ski boot in the seventh grade.

When I got outside, Ranger Rob was showing Randy and Sabs how the bindings on their boots worked. It wasn't too difficult to learn. The boots were really light, almost like shoes, and you clipped the toe into the binding on the ski. We practiced putting them on and taking them off a few times, and then Ranger Rob showed us where to join our class.

"I think I'll carry these," Randy said, hoisting her skis up on her shoulder.

"Good idea!" Sabs agreed.

I decided to try to ski over, since it wasn't

very far. I was doing okay, almost gliding across the snow. But the class was meeting at the bottom of a small slope. I put my skis parallel and started going forward. *Just go slowly*, I thought. *then nothing can go wrong*. But before I knew it, my skis had crossed and I had sped up beyond my control. I felt myself falling sideways, and then my body swung around and I slid down the rest of the way — headfirst!

When I landed at the bottom, there were about ten kids waiting there, and they all started to clap.

"Bravo," I heard a strange voice say. I looked up and saw a tall man, with dark brown hair, tanned skin, and dark eyes, standing above me.

"Put your skis parallel, and I will help you up," he said, and I realized he had a foreign accent that I didn't recognize. I tried to do what he said, and I swung my skis to one side and put them parallel. He reached out his hand to pull me up. But as he pulled I started sliding forward, and I pulled him down instead. The whole group started laughing. I was so embarrassed, I was ready to cry. I decided to unclip my bindings and stand up on my own two feet. Randy and Sabrina walked over to me.

"Are you okay, Al?" Sabs asked anxiously.

"Yes, I'm fine," I said, totally embarrassed.

"I'm glad you're okay, Al," Randy said, helping me brush the snow off my clothes. "Not a bad start. Not a bad start at all!" Randy usually knows just how to make me feel better.

"Boys and girls," the man I had pulled down began. "My name is Alain Rauscher, and I will be your teacher of skiing here today. I am an Alpine skier from France, so excuse please my English."

"Wow! A French skier, here?" Randy whispered excitedly. "That's pretty cool."

Alain brushed the snow off the back of his jacket and looked over at me with a smile.

"What this mademoiselle has just shown to us is most important to begin the cross-country skiing. That is — how to fall."

A few kids started laughing again, but Alain continued, looking serious. "You must always fall as —" He paused and turned to me again. "What was your name?" he said.

My heart must have skipped a beat, and

my stomach tightened.

"Al, uh, Allison," I stuttered.

"What Allison has shown to us is the correct way to fall. In the cross-country skiing, you must always fall to the side. This way, you do not hurt yourself."

"You're a natural," Randy said, giving me a nudge.

Alain had us all line up, and he led us down a flat trail, instructing us on the proper motion. He told us that cross-country skiing is almost a cross between ice skating and running. After a while I really felt like I was getting the hang of it. I was even ready to try the little hill again. Just as I was approaching the top, Alain came up beside me.

"You are looking much better," he said.

"Thank you," I gulped.

"I will show you how to slow yourself down on the hill," he told me. "Watch."

He went ahead of me and turned the front of his skis slightly in, so that they weren't parallel anymore. He was in complete control as he went slowly down the hill.

I followed behind him, keeping my weight on the inside edge of my skis and keeping my toes pointed in. It worked! I went more slowly than I had the first time, and I never lost my balance.

"I think you are a very good student," he told me. "Or maybe I am a very good teacher," he added with a wink. "But now I must help the little redhead. She is not so much a natural!"

I looked over to where he was pointing and saw Sabs facedown in the snow. I decided to try the hill again. When I made my way to the top, I found Randy there, about to ski down.

"Hey, Ran. Wait up," I called to her.

"This is great!" she exclaimed when I caught up. "I'll race you down!"

"No way!" I said very definitely. There was nothing she could say or do that was going to get me to race downhill after I had already made such a fool of myself.

"Come on, Al!" she cried. "Ready, set, go." Before I knew it, she was going straight down the hill. I followed behind at my controlled pace. I couldn't believe how fast she was going. I also couldn't believe that she didn't fall at the bottom. She just kept going straight ahead until she came to a stop.

"That was great," I said, when I caught up with her.

"Well, as long as I can go in a straight line, I figure I'll stop eventually," she said.

"Poor Sabs," I said, pointing. Sabs was on the ground again, her skis crossed behind her.

"Let's go help her," Randy said. She skied off toward Sabrina, who had managed to stand up, and I followed right behind. I watched as Randy glided up behind Sabrina and grabbed her around the waist, knocking her off balance. She fell into Randy, pushing her down right into me. Before I knew it, the three of us were in one big heap in the snow, laughing hysterically!

By the time we got to our cabin that night after dinner, we were totally exhausted and could hardly move. We were even too tired to fight with Stacy and her gang about taking all the best bunks. We just changed into our nightgowns and got into our sleeping bags.

All of us except for Stacy, that is. She hadn't brought a sleeping bag. She had pink sheets and two matching pink blankets. Her bed was carefully made. Randy whispered to me that she was surprised that Stacy knew how to make her own bed.

She took the longest time to get ready. She brushed her long blond hair at least a hundred times and then braided it so that it would be wavy the next day. By the time she was ready to get into bed, we were all practically asleep.

"Ahhh!" she screamed, startling us all. "Who did this to my bed?"

"What's wrong?" Eva asked. She jumped out of her own bunk and ran over to Stacy.

"I can't get my feet down past here!" Stacy shrieked.

"You mean you made your bed wrong?" Sabs asked innocently.

"I mean someone short-sheeted my bed!" Stacy yelled. She looked like she was about to kill somebody. "Who did it?"

"Girls!" Miss Miller called from the next room. "Lights out, and no more talking!"

"I want to know who did this," Stacy repeated in a whisper.

No one said anything, but I could feel my bunk shaking. I was in the top bunk, and Randy was in the bottom. I looked over the edge, and I could see Randy lying facedown, her head in her pillow, laughing uncontrollably. Katie sat up in bed and looked over at our bunk. Suddenly she winked at me.

"Maybe some of the boys sneaked in here at dinner," Katie suggested quietly. "They've been a total pain since we got here."

"Yeah," Laurel agreed. "I'll bet Nick did it because he was so mad at you for ignoring him before."

"Well, I'll get him back for this!" Stacy mumbled as she remade her bed. Sabs, Katie, Randy, and I couldn't help laughing into our pillows. Finally, Stacy switched off the light, and we all fell asleep.

1

Chapter Six

Stacy woke up in a terrible mood the next morning. She kept grumbling about Nick Robbins, and each time she did, I saw Randy biting her lip, trying not to laugh.

After we finished eating our breakfast — bowls of cold, soggy oatmeal — Ranger Rhonda and Ranger Rob got up to speak.

"Not these clowns again," Randy groaned.

"I think you should listen, Ranger Randy," Katie teased, and the whole table started laughing.

"If we could have your attention!" Ranger Rhonda said enthusiastically. "We have a real treat for all of you!"

"Now that you have all learned the basics of cross-country skiing," Ranger Rob continued, "we'd like to send you all on an activity that will help you discover the beauty of the Eagle Mountain area."

Ranger Rhonda smiled brightly and picked up where Ranger Rob had left off. I wondered if they could read each other's mind. "We're sending you off on a scavenger hunt," she finished.

A murmur ran through the crowd. I waited.

Ranger Rob rubbed his hands together. "But this is no ordinary scavenger hunt," he said mysteriously. "Because this scavenger hunt takes place on skis!"

I heard a few groans, a sigh from Sabrina, and a couple of cheers.

Ranger Rhonda held up her hand for silence. "We're asking each cabin to divide up into two groups," she said.

"That shouldn't be too hard for our cabin," Randy mumbled.

"Yeah," Katie whispered, "we're already divided into two groups."

"Each cabin will take the trail with the same number as their cabin," said Ranger Rhonda.

"I guess we're on trail fifty-three," Randy said, and for some reason, I felt my stomach tighten as that chilling, nervous feeling hit me again.

"Your job," Ranger Rob explained, as he held up a green ribbon for us to see, "is to collect as many of these green ribbons as you can. We have tied them on the trees along the trails. The group that collects the most ribbons will be our first-place winners. The first group to make it back to the lodge will be our grand-prize champions."

"Now before we go over to the ski room, table by table, and get suited up," Ranger Rhonda said with another smile, "I want you all to remember how important it is to stay on your trail. Some of the trails are old and very dangerous and have been closed off." Another murmur went around the room as people got in line to get their ski equipment.

Finally, our table was called to get our gear. As we were waiting on line, Alfie the dog came trotting up to us, and I scratched him behind the ears.

We took our skis outside to put them on. Stacy, Eva, Laurel, and B.Z. were already out there snapping their boots into their bindings.

"Well, it looks like the competition finally made it," said Stacy, pulling on her pink ski gloves.

"Doesn't look like it'll be much of a contest," sneered Eva.

"Randy, that's an interesting ski suit you're wearing," Laurel commented.

I looked at Randy and realized that she was wearing a pretty unusual outfit for a skier. In addition to her usual black leather jacket, she had on these stretch pants with leopard spots all over them, and a pair of earmuffs that looked like bears' heads.

"Yeah," B.Z. said with a laugh. "I hope you don't meet up with any hunters."

Katie had just finished snapping Randy's skis onto her boots for her, but I guess Randy hadn't really noticed, because she started to head right toward B.Z. and the others. As soon as she did, her ski tips crossed over each other and she began to lose her balance. The next moment, her legs were completely tangled, and she fell in a heap on the snow.

Stacy, Eva, Laurel, and B.Z. started laughing even louder.

"Well, like I said, it doesn't look like these guys are going to be much competition for us," said Stacy, pushing off toward the trail.

"Good luck!" called Eva, gliding after her.

"You're going to need it!"

"Randy, you shouldn't let them get to you like that," said Katie, once they were gone.

"I can't help it," said Randy. "They make me so mad I could spit."

Katie reached out to try to help Randy back to her feet, but Randy just ended up pulling Katie down on top of her, and in a moment all four of their skis were tangled together. I guess Sabs and I must have started toward them at the same moment, because the next thing I knew, one of her skis had slid over the front of mine. When she tried to move it back off, she lost her balance. At the last minute, she grabbed my elbow, and we both ended up down in the snow.

Suddenly, we heard someone laughing. For a minute, I thought Stacy had come back, but it was Randy, who was still hopelessly tangled up with Katie.

"I can't believe this," she managed to get out between giggles. "We're not even at the trail yet, and already I've caused a major accident!"

When Katie heard this, she started to laugh, too, and soon we were all lying helplessly in the snow, laughing so hard we could barely breathe.

Somehow, we managed to untangle our skis, poles, arms, and legs. But by that time Stacy's group had a big head start.

"They're probably so far ahead of us, there won't be any of those green ribbons left by the time we get out there," I said.

"Now what are we going to do?" wailed Katie.

"I think I've got an idea," said Sabrina, looking at the map of ski trails that was posted near the door of the equipment shack. "Look, there's another trail, a shorter one, that meets up with number fifty-three. See it? It's in yellow and black, right in the middle of all those green ones. If we start off on that trail, I'm sure we can cut off Stacy's group right up therewhere they connect."

"Totally cool idea, Sabs!" said Randy. "Let's do it!"

"Sounds good to me," said Katie.

"But Ranger Rhonda said to stay on our cabin trail," I said doubtfully.

Randy, Sabs, and Katie looked at me with disappointed expressions on their faces.

"Can't we bend the rules just a little?" asked Sabrina pleadingly.

"Yeah, it's only a shortcut," said Randy. "Look. It's not one of those dangerous trails."

"Come on, Al," said Katie. "We're just going to catch up. Nothing will happen."

They all stood there looking at me. I knew they wouldn't go if I really didn't want to, but I couldn't stand disappointing them, so I finally said okay.

I slid my skis along in the snow, and after a moment I got into the rhythm of it. Maybe Alain had been right. Maybe I was a natural.

I looked around. There wasn't a cloud in the sky, and the bright sun made the snow shine. It seemed like everything around us was sparkling. There were even little ledges of snow piled up on the tops of all the branches.

The snow looked so beautiful against the dark branches that I thought of a poem by Robert Frost that we had read in English class called, "Stopping by Woods on a Snowy Evening." I took a deep breath of cold air and thought maybe this trip was going to turn out all right after all.

Chapter Seven

When we entered the woods, Katie was in the lead. Sabrina was behind her, followed by Randy, and I was at the end. The trail was narrow, so there was really only enough room for one pair of skis at a time.

At first Sabs lost her balance a lot, and a couple of times she even slipped and fell, but after a few minutes she seemed to be getting the hang of it. She was certainly doing a whole lot better than the day before. I guess falling down isn't as much fun when you don't have a gorgeous French ski instructor to help you up.

We were all gliding along pretty quickly when Katie called out suddenly and the line stopped.

"What's the matter?" I heard Randy ask.

"What happened?" I chimed in. "Why did we stop?"

It was Sabrina who answered. "It's a tree!" she yelled back to us.

Randy turned to look at me and shrugged

her shoulders.

What could be the problem with a tree? I wondered. There must have been hundreds of them all around us.

"You guys, maybe you should come up here and look at this!" Katie called back to us.

Randy stepped sideways up onto the bank of snow to the left, and I stepped up onto the bank of snow to the right. We slid carefully up to where Katie and Sabrina were standing. Right away I saw what the problem was. A large tree trunk lay across the trail, blocking our path.

"Wow," Randy commented.

"It must have been struck by lightning," said Katie.

"But that's strange," I said. "Lightning usually only strikes in warmer weather."

"So?" asked Sabrina. "It probably happened a few months ago or something, right?"

"But think about it," I said. "Wouldn't someone have reported it, and shouldn't the rangers or somebody have cleared it away by now?"

"Gee, you're probably right," agreed Katie. "It is strange."

"Well, how are we supposed to get past it?" Sabs asked.

"I know how I'm getting by," Randy announced. She bent down and began to unsnap her bindings.

Suddenly I thought of something. "Hey, Randy," I said. "Be careful. Since our skis have just been gliding along the top, there's no way to tell how deep this snow is, especially on the side where you are —"

But I guess I was a little late. Before I had even finished my sentence, Randy stepped off her skis and into the snow, sinking all the way up to her knees.

She looked at us, shrugged, lifted her skis and poles onto one shoulder, and pulled herself over the tree trunk.

I was beginning to think that we should turn back and try to take trail fifty-three after all, or just give up on the scavenger hunt completely. But Sabrina was already taking off her skis and getting ready to follow Randy. Katie bent down to unsnap her bindings, too.

I realized I had very little choice unless I wanted to turn back by myself. So I took off my skis and stepped down into the snow.

It wasn't easy climbing over that big snow-covered tree trunk with our skis and poles in our hands. But we all made it, and managed to put our skis back on once we were on the other side.

We continued along the trail. This time Sabrina was in the lead, and I was right behind her. Katie followed me, and Randy was in the back. Sabrina stopped suddenly, and I heard her exclaim, "I can't believe this." I couldn't see past her to find out what the problem was.

"What is it?" Katie called from behind me.

"It's a stream," Sabs called out to her.

"That's okay," Katie reassured her. "They have those on a lot of trails. Just ski straight across the footbridge."

"What footbridge?"

Katie sighed, climbed up on a snowbank, and started to slide past me on her skis. I heard Sabs say, "Well, I'm not taking off my skis again!" And then I saw Sabrina begin to move forward.

The next thing I heard was a crack and a yelp. I rushed ahead to see what had happened. Katie was right beside me, and I could hear Randy hurrying to catch up.

What I saw was Sabrina on the other side of a half-frozen little stream. She was sitting in the snow, her ski poles sticking out in different directions. The worst part was that the tip of her right ski had broken off. The missing tip, a piece about a foot long, was beside her.

"Sabs! What happened?" Katie yelled.

"Are you all right?" I asked.

"Yeah," she answered. "I'm fine."

Randy came up behind us. "Oh, Sabs," she said, "you look like a broken windmill!"

"What am I going to do?" wailed Sabrina. "I broke a ski! The rangers are going to be so mad!"

"Sabrina, try to relax," I said. "The important thing is that you didn't break anything else."

"Yeah," said Randy, "like a leg!"

"That's right," said Katie. "Thank goodness you're not hurt."

"How did you do this?" Randy asked.

"Well, like I said, there was no bridge. I really didn't want to have to take my skis off again, and they looked so long, and the stream looked pretty narrow. Anyway, I thought that maybe I could sort of use my skis as a bridge and just sort of ski from one bank to the other."

"Oh, Sabs," said Katie. "Skis aren't that strong."

"I found that out," said Sabrina. "I put the tips of my skis on the other side, but I guess I was too heavy for them, because one of them just snapped. I'm just glad I managed to get to the other side at all."

"You guys!" Katie exclaimed. "Look over here!"

"What is it?" I asked, not knowing what Katie was pointing at.

"See these black markers on the tree?" said Katie. "Those are trail markers. I think the trail continues on this side of the stream. I'll bet there's a bridge farther down."

"You mean we don't have to cross?" Randy asked, excited.

"I'm not coming back across," Sabs cried out. "No way. Besides, there are yellow markers on the trees over here."

"I wonder which trail meets up with trail fifty-three?" I said. "Katie, where's the trail map?"

"I don't know, Al, I thought you had it," answered Katie.

"Great," said Sabrina, moaning. "Now we're lost for sure!"

"Why don't we follow the black trail until we find a bridge?" Randy suggested. "Then we can come back on the other side of the river and pick up Sabs."

"No way," Katie declared. "We are not going to split up. Why don't we just take off our skis again? We'll follow the yellow markers. They've got to lead somewhere."

"Well," said Randy with a sigh, "here we go again. Off with the skis, I guess."

"Sabrina, I'm going to hand my skis over first," I said. "I don't think I can get across if I have to carry them."

I held my skis and poles across the stream, and Sabrina stretched out her arms and managed to reach them.

I climbed down the first snowbank and jumped over the stream. It wasn't very wide, so it was really pretty easy for me with my long legs. But as I was climbing up the bank on the other side, my foot slipped on the snow and landed back down in the water. I quickly pulled it out, and Sabrina gave me a hand climbing up.

Together we helped Katie and Randy get their skis across and pulled them up the bank.

We put our skis on and continued down the trail, with me in the lead this time. After a while I began to realize something. As I slid my skis along the snow, I noticed that the tracks they made were the first ones on the trail. I stopped for a moment and waited for the others to catch up.

"I've been thinking," I said. "There is definitely something funny about this trail. There aren't any other ski tracks here but ours."

"So? That's because we're the only people here."

"No," I said. "Shouldn't someone else have used this trail besides us since the last snowfall?"

"So maybe it's just an unpopular trail," said Randy.

"Yeah," I said, "maybe. But why is it so unpopular? I mean, if this is really a trail, why wasn't that tree trunk cleared away? And what happened to the footbridge?"

"This is creepy," said Sabrina.

"And there's more," I went on. "Where's the turnoff where this trail is supposed to meet up with the other one? It seems to me like we've already gone much farther than we should have."

"That's right," Katie agreed. "Remember the map? This trail was supposed to meet up with the other one pretty quickly, wasn't it?"

"So what should we do?" asked Sabrina." Turn around and go back?"

"And lose the scavenger hunt to Stacy and her gang? No way!" said Randy.

"There are more important things than the scavenger hunt," I said softly.

"Really," said Katie, beginning to worry. "I mean what if we get even more lost, and it gets dark, and —"

"Katie," Randy said, trying to calm her down. "It's only eleven o'clock. It's not exactly sunset yet!"

That was true. But suddenly I realized that the sun was on our right, which meant we were headed north. The trail we were trying to meet up with should be to the east. There was definitely something wrong. And I was getting that creepy feeling again. I kept picturing Eagle Feather wandering around in the woods, looking for his son and wife. Maybe his spirit did haunt the woods. Maybe that's why we were having such bad luck!

"You guys, I'm pretty sure we missed the turnoff to trail fifty-three," I said.

"But where were the markers for it?" asked Katie. "There are usually little markers on the trees to let you know what trail you're on." She looked around for a moment. "Come to think of it, where are the markers for *this* trail?" she asked.

"Oh, I'm scared," said Sabrina unhappily.

"What do you think, Al?" Randy asked. "Should we turn back?"

I thought for a moment. "No," I said, "we must be more than halfway by now. I don't think it would make sense to turn back."

"Okay," said Katie, "then let's just keep going."

We continued along the trail in silence. I looked at Sabrina. She must have been having a pretty tough time skiing on her broken ski. She kept losing her balance and falling, and her back was covered with snow. I started to think, *What would we do if it did get dark and we still hadn't reached the end of the trail?* I definitely didn't want to be lost in the woods at night.

After a little while, the trees on my right thinned out, and I realized we were skiing along the edge of a small cliff. About five feet below, I could see a river. It was mostly frozen over, but there were still patches of moving water. It made me shiver just looking at that frozen water. I could picture myself sliding all the way down the hill and having to carry my skis all the way up again through the deep snow.

I skied as close as I could to the trees on my left. At one point, I had to grab a branch to steady myself. I could hear Katie, who was skiing right behind me, gasp as I almost lost my balance.

"Ugh," said Sabrina as she arrived at the scary part. "I don't think I can take this. I'm scared of heights!"

"Just stay as close to the trees on the left as you can," I called back to her. "Try not to get too close to the edge!"

"It's not that much farther, Sabs!" Katie called out.

Pretty soon the trail swerved back in among the trees, away from the edge of the cliff. I have to admit I was pretty relieved. I leaned against a tree and took a deep breath.

In a moment, Katie came gliding along the trail.

"Boy, that was scary, wasn't it?" she said. "For a minute, I didn't think I was going to make it."

"Yeah," I agreed. "Hey, where's Sabs and Randy? They were right behind us a minute ago. Do you think they're okay? It's taking them a while."

Katie looked at me with a worried expression. "We have to go back and find them," she said.

When we got back to the cliff, Sabrina and Randy were making their way along the edge.

Sabrina looked really scared. Her eyes were squeezed shut, and she was moving her skis forward about an inch at a time. Randy was skiing alongside her, on her right, putting herself between Sabrina and the cliff. I could hear her leading Sabrina along, coaxing her gently.

"Come on, Sabs, that's it, you can do it," Randy was saying.

"Oh, Randy, be careful!" Katie yelled. "You're right on the edge!"

"Whoa!" Randy cried out. She tried to balance herself on her right pole, but instead the wrist strap broke and the pole went sliding down the hill to the frozen river below. Luckily, Sabs had grabbed a tree and was able to hold on to the sleeve of Randy's leather jacket with her other hand. Randy quickly regained her balance, and we all heaved a sigh of relief.

The amazing thing was that Randy looked just as frightened as Sabrina. And I don't think I had ever seen Randy look frightened before. She's always really good at appearing confident, even when she's not.

Finally, Sabs and Randy inched their way up to where Katie and I were standing.

"That was really close!" Randy exclaimed.

"You must have been so scared," I said.

"Scared?" Randy said. "Me? Are you kidding? No way."

Katie and I looked at each other and began to giggle.

"Well, you really saved me," Sabs said gratefully. And I could tell that we were all relieved. I looked around and took a deep breath. It really was so beautiful there. Everything was white, and it was so quiet, except for the sound of the river flowing where it hadn't frozen over. The air was fresh, and the sky was clear. I just wished we knew where we were going!

Then I noticed something.

"Look!" I said. "The trail goes downhill from here, and it bends to the right. That's west, the direction of the lodge. I think we're getting there!"

"All right!" Randy exclaimed.

"But how is Randy ever going to be able to ski downhill with only one pole?" Katie asked.

Randy grinned. "A hill? No problem!" she said. "Who needs poles?" We all looked at her. "It's like skateboarding, right? You don't use poles with a skateboard. All this time I knew that there was something holding me back with this skiing stuff. Now I know — it was the poles. Now watch this and you'll see a real pro!"

Sabrina, Katie, and I stared at her in disbelief. We knew Randy was a little wild, but this seemed crazy.

Before anyone could stop her, she had taken off down the hill, her body swaying easily back and forth with the curves, and her one ski pole waving wildly in the air above her head.

Katie looked at me and shrugged. "Well, here goes," she said, giving herself a big push with her poles and flying down the hill, around the bend, and out of sight.

I was next. I stood uneasily at the top of the hill and looked down. It wasn't a steep hill, but it was definitely steeper than anything I had ever skied down, and it had at least one sharp bend that I could see. But there was certainly no turning back now, so I took a deep breath and pushed off.

I kept my knees bent and leaned forward over my skis. I skied slowly, in the controlled way that Alain had taught me. I managed to make it around the first bend and began to relax. It felt great, actually, gliding along through the woods like that, feeling the wind blowing back my hair, and the icy air on my face.

Occasionally, I could see the back of Katie's parka as she turned the corners ahead of me. I knew Sabrina must be close behind me.

Then I heard Randy let out a shriek from down below. At first I was sure she had broken her leg or something, but she kept yelling. I realized they were yells of happiness. A few moments later her voice was joined by Katie's.

Suddenly, I shot out of the woods and into a clearing. There were Randy and Katie, standing side by side. There, just a few yards beyond them, was the lodge! I heard myself cheer out loud. I slid to a stop behind Randy and Katie and raised my ski poles to the sky in relief. Somewhere in the distance I could hear Alfie barking.

The next thing I knew, Sabrina came crashing out of the woods. She had all her weight on the ski that wasn't broken, and she was obviously completely out of control. She was headed right for us. We tried frantically to get out of her way, but we couldn't move fast enough, and Sabs smashed right into us. For what seemed like the millionth time that day, we were all in a heap in the snow, but I couldn't think of any place I'd rather be.

Chapter Eight

I warmed my toes by the fire and watched Katie as she tried to balance the tray of hot chocolate she was carrying toward us. It felt great to put on dry clothes and have some lunch, but I still hadn't warmed up completely, and I was glad just to be lounging by the fire.

"Okay," Sabrina admitted. "So maybe it wasn't such a great idea, so maybe we didn't win the scavenger hunt."

"Sabs, we didn't even really *go* on the scavenger hunt," Randy pointed out, making us all laugh.

"I couldn't care less about the dumb old scavenger hunt," Katie said, putting down the tray in front of us. "I'm just glad we made it back alive."

"Yeah," said Randy. "But I still can't believe Miss Miller and Ranger Rob and Ranger Rhonda were so mad at us. All that screaming and stuff got on my nerves."

"We never should have taken that trail

without permission," I said.

"Well," Sabrina huffed, "how were we supposed to know that the trail was for expert skiers only?"

"Sabs, it said it right on the bottom of the map," Katie pointed out. "Green trails are for beginners, blue are intermediate, yellow are advanced, and black are expert."

"Well, who has time to read all that small print when you're on a scavenger hunt?" Sabrina said.

"What was the trail like?" Nick asked. He and a lot of the other kids had come over to hear about our adventure.

"Well, the worst part was the cliff," Randy began. "There was this seventy-foot drop-off to one side —"

"Randy, it wasn't seventy feet," Katie cut in, but it didn't matter. Everyone was really interested in Randy's story. Stacy, Laurel, Eva, and B.Z. may have won the scavenger hunt, but we were definitely the ones getting all the attention. All through lunch they tried to brag about how they brought back every single green ribbon from their trail, more than anyone in the whole history of the Eagle Mountain

Scavenger Hunt. But most people gathered around us to hear our story.

"So, you ladies are ready now to do the real Alpine skiing," Alain said, coming over to us.

"We'll race you anytime," Sabrina said, blushing.

I laughed along with the others, but I was pretty sure that we had just barely managed to make it out of a dangerous situation.

That afternoon we had a choice of skiing some more, going on a nature walk on snowshoes, or staying in the lodge for slides and an ecology lecture with Miss Miller. Katie, Randy, Sabs, and I had done enough skiing for one day, so we all chose to stay inside. And it was the right decision, because the lecture was pretty short. We even had enough time to visit some of the other cabins and hang out a while before dinner.

After dinner, we all gathered around the big fireplace in the lodge's main room, waiting for the evening activity.

Suddenly Sabrina grabbed my arm.

"Here comes Greg," she said quickly. "I wish he would sit with us, and not with Sam and his friends! What should I do?"

Randy stood up. "No problem. Watch this," she said to Sabrina. "Yo! Jason! Nick! Sam! Come sit over here!"

Sam, Nick, and Jason looked around. When Sam saw Randy, he gave her the thumbs-up sign, and the three of them stood up and started to walk over to us.

"Hey, Greg!" Nick called as he was walking across the room. "Come on, we're sitting over here!"

Greg nodded and headed our way.

Meanwhile, Sabrina's face was turning very red.

"Oh, no," she said in a panic, "now he's coming to sit here!"

Randy looked exasperated. "Sabs, isn't that what you wanted?" she asked.

"Yes, but what am I going to say to him?"

"Just act natural," Katie advised. "Don't worry about it too much or you'll seem really nervous."

"You're right," said Sabrina. "*Young Chic* says guys like girls who aren't afraid to be themselves. The problem is, I can't remember how to be myself when Greg is around."

Just then we were interrupted by Ranger

Rhonda, who was standing in the center of the room and ringing what looked like a giant cowbell. She was wearing a white turtleneck, navy blue pants, and the same blue-and-white moon boots.

"Attention! Attention, everybody!" she called just as Nick, Jason, Sam, and Greg sat down on the floor behind us.

Ranger Rhonda stopped ringing her bell. "I think we are all ready for another big tradition here on Eagle Mountain," she announced. "It's time for the ghost story!"

A cheer went up from the room, along with a few howls and shrieks from the boys behind us. I sighed. The last thing I wanted to hear was a ghost story.

"Ranger Rob, would you lower the lights, please?" Rhonda asked sweetly.

The lights began to dim, and people began howling, shrieking, and making scary noises.

Ranger Rhonda rang her cowbell again. "Now, now, hold it down, boys and girls!" she called out. "There will be plenty of scary stuff to go around when you hear the spine-tingling story of the Ghost of Eagle Mountain, as told by our own Ranger Rob!"

I think my heart must have skipped a beat as Ranger Rhonda made her announcement, and I let out a gasp. Suddenly I thought about the legend of Eagle Feather. Did that have something to do with Ranger Rob's story? I shivered. I definitely wasn't sure I wanted to hear it.

Rhonda rang the bell again, and the crowd waited as Ranger Rob walked to the center of the room. It was no surprise at all to see that he was wearing a white turtleneck, navy pants, and blue-and-white moon boots. He cleared his throat and then was quiet for a minute, waiting for the room to become absolutely silent.

"I am about to tell you a very old story," he began. "It is also a true story. It is part of the history of Eagle Mountain, and I want you all to listen carefully."

I was hardly breathing. I was waiting to see if he was about to tell the legend Nooma had taught me.

"I don't know how many of you know this," he continued. "But there used to be a tribe of Indians living right here on this mountain."

And then I realized that if the ghost story was about Indians on this mountain, it must be the legend of Eagle Feather. Suddenly, I felt goosebumps on my arms.

"Yes," Ranger Rob went on, "they were a frightening bunch. And the most frightening of them all was their chief."

Frightening? I thought. *What was frightening about Eagle Feather*? I hate when people make up things about the Chippewa people or other Native Americans without really knowing anything about them.

"Now, I can tell you all the name of this particular Indian chief, but if I do, I'm going to have to say it very, very softly. Because if he hears us talking about him, he will get very, very angry, and then there's no telling what might happen." He paused. "Do you want to hear his name?" he asked.

"Yes!" yelled the kids.

"Tell us the guy's name!" I heard Greg call out.

Ranger Rob lowered his voice. "His name," he said, looking around the room as if he expected to be attacked at any moment, "his name . . . is Flying Eagle."

"Eagle Feather," I whispered, correcting him.

"What?" asked Katie, turning to me.

"Nothing," I said.

"Yes, Flying Eagle was truly terrible when he was alive on this mountain. It is said that he captured hundreds of settlers and used their skulls for money!"

There were a few gasps and whispers. I could feel a couple of kids glance my way, but I pretended not to notice. *That isn't true!* I thought. *Eagle Feather was kind and good. He only tried to protect his people!*

"But the legend goes on to say that Flying Eagle is even more terrible and frightening now that he is dead," said Ranger Rob dramatically. "Many people still believe that Flying Eagle roams the mountain at night, looking for victims to capture."

I felt Katie move a little closer to me.

"Aaaghh, I think he got me!" yelled Greg, pretending to strangle himself.

"Shut up, Loggins," Nick hissed.

Ranger Rob went on. "Listen closely, boys and girls. Flying Eagle left his people and disappeared into the woods a long time ago, so long ago that he ought to be dead. He wandered around this mountain for fifty-three days, and then he just disappeared. No one knows what he did for those fifty-three days, but he was never heard from again. Flying Eagle is said to have strengthened his magical powers so that he is still very much alive. If you listen carefully to the wind at night here on Eagle Mountain, you can sometimes hear him howling."

Behind us, Greg began to howl.

I closed my eyes. I couldn't believe what I was hearing. Ranger Rob was telling the story of Eagle Feather, only he was telling it all wrong! Eagle Feather hadn't been terrible and frightening. He was a man who had fought to defend his tribe, his home, and his family. Why did the rangers have to make him sound like all of those stereotypical Indians that they all show in the movies? Why didn't they tell us about Running Deer and Little Wolf?

Eagle Feather and his tribe were Native Americans — these hills had been their home years before the settlers came to Minnesota. Their story should be told truthfully and with respect. I was starting to get angry.

"And if you do hear the ghost of Eagle Mountain, beware, for when he's howling, he's angry. And when he's angry, there's no telling what may happen!" said Ranger Rob.

There was a gasp from the audience. Then the lights went back on and Ranger Rob smiled at us.

"Well, I hope you're not all too frightened to make it back to your cabins," said Ranger Rhonda. "Pleasant dreams!"

We stood up and began putting on our jackets.

"Some ghost story," said Greg. "What a joke."

"It wasn't a joke," I told him quickly.

"It *was* kind of spooky," said Sabrina.

"What's the matter, girls?" Greg teased. "Scared to walk back in the dark? Afraid that a wild Indian's going to get you?" He let out a few loud whoops and started dancing around. Sam, Nick, and Jason turned and stared at him.

I glared at him, furious. But I don't think he even noticed.

I had forgotten all about Randy's temper. Before anyone knew what was happening, she was standing face-to-face with Greg. "Hey, clod, the story of Flying Eagle is part of the history of Native Americans. Who are you to make it into a joke?"

"It's just a dumb story about some dumb Indian," said Greg. "Anyway, why should you care?"

"Because Allison here is my best friend and she's a Native American. And I don't think she's dumb and I don't laugh at other people's history, that's why!" exclaimed Randy loudly.

"Yeah, well I think the whole thing's stupid," said Greg, turning really red. "Besides, you can't tell me what to do!"

I couldn't say anything, I was still too angry. I wanted to tell them all the *real* story. But not with this Greg character around.

"Come on, Allison," said Katie, pulling my arm. "Let's get away from this bingo head!"

"That's right," exclaimed Sabrina. "I don't want to be around people who act like jerks!" Sam and Jason and Nick just stood there with embarrassed looks on their faces.

Randy, Katie, Sabrina, and I turned and walked away from the four boys toward our cabin.

"I hope you don't mind if I say this, Sabs,"

Katie started.

"What?" asked Sabrina.

"Well," said Katie, "I think Greg was awful back there."

"Really," Randy agreed.

"I know," said Sabrina thoughtfully. "I guess you never know with people. He seemed like such a nice guy —"

We were approaching the cabin and suddenly Sabrina let out a little yelp.

"Sabrina, what is it?" said Randy.

"Are you okay?" asked Katie.

"What's wrong?" I asked.

"L-l-look," she stammered. "Above the door! Look at the number."

. There was a moment of silence, and then Randy said, "I get it. Wow, that is kind of spooky. Fifty-three."

Sabrina gasped. "Oh, my gosh, it's a sign. I know all about these things. Number fifty-three! That's how many days Flying Eagle was in the woods before he disappeared."

"It's just a strange coincidence," said Katie shakily after a minute. She stomped up the steps and reached for the door.

I followed the others inside. Now they

knew about the significance of number fifty-three as well. I couldn't help but think about all the strange things that had happened: first the bus breaking down, then getting lost in the woods, and then Greg Loggins acting like such a jerk and making us so mad. I couldn't help wondering what was going to happen next, but I wasn't so sure I wanted to find out.

Chapter Nine

"I wonder where our other cabin mates are?" asked Katie, smoothing her sleeping bag over her bunk

"Maybe a ghost got them," Randy joked, flopping down on her bunk.

I had just started changing for bed when I heard a funny noise coming from outside.

"Oooooooo. . ."

Sabrina looked up from the sweater she was folding. "Did you hear that?" she asked.

"Ooooooo. . .oooooooooo. . ."

"There it is again," Sabrina whispered.

"What was that?" asked Randy, sitting up.

"I heard it, too," said Katie.

I could feel that familiar tingle on the back of my neck. I didn't like this at all.

Suddenly the cabin door flew open, and Stacy, Eva, B.Z., and Laurel burst in.

"Oh, my gosh!" said Stacy breathlessly.

"There's something out there," said Eva,

pointing at the door.

"We know," said Sabrina.

"We heard it, too," Katie told them.

The noise started up again. "Oooooo. . . Oooooooo!"

"It's the ghost of Eagle Mountain!" B.Z. wailed.

"Now wait. There's probably a perfectly logical explanation for this," I said, but I realized that my voice was shaking.

"I think it stopped," said Randy.

"Let's look outside," said Katie. "Maybe we can see something."

"Are you kidding?" asked Sabrina.

"No way," said Laurel.

"Maybe Katie's right," said Stacy. "Let's just open the door and look. After all, there are eight of us. What can happen?"

We all crept toward the door in a huddle. A loose floorboard creaked under somebody's foot. Sabs gasped.

Gently, Katie pushed the door open. We could see the steps and the snow-covered path in front of the cabin. Beyond that there was only darkness.

Then it started again.

"Ooooooooo!"

We grabbed for each other's arms.

"I don't like this one bit," said Sabrina. I couldn't have agreed more.

"Let's go back inside," Laurel pleaded.

"Hold on," said Katie.

Just then four dark shapes went rushing past. We all screamed and scrambled to get back into the cabin.

No sooner had we made it inside than the door burst open again and the same four shapes came running in after us. I recognized the shapes as four sleeping bags with human feet.

"Oooooooh!" said a blue sleeping bag, and the other ones started to snicker.

Sabrina's face turned bright red.

"I know that laugh," she announced. "And I know that sleeping bag, too, because it matches mine!" She marched over to the blue sleeping bag and yanked it down. Underneath was her twin brother, Sam.

The three other sleeping bags came off, and Jason, Nick, and Greg appeared, laughing and clutching their stomachs.

"Ooooooo!" said Greg between bouts of

laughter. "Watch out, I'm a ghost!"

Sabrina was fuming. "That wasn't funny and you know it!"

"You should have seen the looks on your faces," said Sam, practically choking with laughter. We just looked at each other.

"Yeah, yeah, very funny act," said Randy. "But the show's over now, so why don't you guys just get out of here?"

The boys looked at each other, still laughing, and headed for the door.

"Okay," Greg called back to us, "but watch out for ghosts!"

"Oooooo! Oooooo!" said the others.

"They are so immature!" said Stacy, flipping her hair over her shoulders and walking toward her bunk.

"Really," said Eva.

"Hey, where's Miss Miller, anyway?" asked Sabrina. "Isn't she supposed to be here watching out for stuff like this?"

"I'll bet I know who she's with," said Randy jokingly.

"You're crazy!" said Katie, rolling up her sweater into a ball and throwing it at Randy. "Do you really think Miss Miller and Mr.

Byrne —"

At that very moment the door opened, and Miss Miller walked in. Katie quickly put her hand over her mouth, and Randy buried her head in the sweater Katie had thrown at her. I could see Randy's shoulders shaking, and I knew she was laughing.

"Well, hello, girls," said Miss Miller, unwinding her plaid scarf from around her neck. "I'm glad to see we all made it back safely."

"Hello, Miss Miller," we said. No one looked at anyone else, and I could tell most of us were trying not to laugh.

Miss Miller looked over at Randy, who still had her head buried in Katie's sweater.

"Is she all right?" she asked.

Katie spoke up. "Uh, yes, Miss Miller. She'll be fine. She was just a little upset by that story that Ranger Rob told tonight," she fibbed.

Miss Miller looked concerned as she pulled her plaid coat off. I couldn't believe my eyes. Under the huge coat was a sweater in a totally different plaid pattern. Unfortunately, Randy looked up just at that moment. Her eyes got real big and she let out a little scream. She got up and ran to the bathroom. "Oh, yes," Miss Miller continued. "A terrible thing, that story. Well, try to forget it and get some sleep." She turned and went into her room.

"Phew," Katie whispered when Miss Miller had closed the door behind her. "That was close!"

Randy came out of the bathroom with her face still red from laughing.

"That's for sure," she said.

We began changing into our nightclothes. Then to my surprise I heard Randy compliment B.Z. on her red-and-white-striped long johns. I guess the ghost story and being frightened by the boys had brought us all a little closer.

I put on my favorite nightgown. It's yellow with a beautiful Indian design which my mother had given me for my birthday. Then I put on my dad's big gold sweater. The sweater smelled just like the fireplace at the lodge, and when I climbed up onto my bunk and snuggled down into my sleeping bag, I began to feel almost cozy. I could hear Miss Miller snoring gently in her room, and as I shut my eyes, I was determined to sleep well on my final night on Eagle Mountain.

"Well, good night, guys," said Katie. Then she pulled the chain on the light in the center of the room and headed toward her bed.

Suddenly a loud howling rang out from the woods — matter of fact, it sounded as if it came from right outside our cabin door!

"What is it?" asked Laurel nervously.

A low moaning sound, almost like a cry, came from outside the cabin.

"It must be the boys again," said Sabrina.

"I can't believe them!" said Stacy.

We heard the sound again. It sounded like someone was hurt.

"They're nuts," said Randy. "Do they really think we're going to fall for that again?"

"That's it," said Sabrina. "I'm getting sick of this. I'm really going to let that Sam have it this time!" She climbed down off her bunk and marched toward the door.

When she pulled open the door, we were all pretty surprised to see Sam, Nick, Jason, and Greg standing out there in their pajamas, down jackets and snow boots. They looked pretty startled, and Sam's arm was raised as if he was just getting ready to pound on our door.

"Sam Wells! Did you honestly think we'd fall for that stupid prank again?" Sabrina demanded.

"We thought it was you guys trying to get us back," Nick explained.

"Of course not," Stacy Hansen called out from her bunk.

Randy jumped down from her bunk. "Well, if it's not you and it's not us," she said, "then who is it?"

Just then we heard the sound again. It was a sort of a howl, more like someone was wailing or crying. I tried not to think about Eagle Feather.

"Are you guys *sure* you're not up to something?" Stacy challenged, pulling on her pink bathrobe and peering out the door behind them.

"How could we make those sounds?" Sam asked. "We're standing right here in front of you."

"It sounds like someone crying," I said.

"Maybe it's the wind," Greg suggested, but he didn't really look like he believed it himself.

"Maybe we should wake Miss Miller up

and. . ."

"No," I said, to my own surprise. "Don't do that. I'll find out what it is." I couldn't help it. I knew I shouldn't go out alone, but I felt something calling to me outside and I had to find out what it was.

"Allison?" Randy asked, walking over to me. "What are you going to do?"

"I'm going to go out and find out what's making that noise."

"No problem, Al, I'll go with you," said Randy.

"No!" I heard myself telling her. "I have to find out by myself."

I heard Sabrina and Katie gasp, and I knew that everybody was staring at me in surprise. I didn't blame them. I was pretty surprised myself.

I found my boots and slipped them on under my long nightgown. Then I put on my down jacket over my sweater and wrapped a scarf around my neck. I was pretty scared of whatever it was that was out there, but I knew I had to do it. Besides, if it did turn out to have anything to do with Eagle Feather, I was the only one there who knew anything about the real story.

"Al, you just can't go off into the woods at night!" Randy exclaimed.

"Look," I said to Randy, "I just *have* to take care of this by myself, *okay*!" Randy looked at me with a surprised and worried expression on her face, but just said, "okay, Al."

Everyone watched as I threw my sleeping bag over my shoulders for extra warmth and stepped out of the cabin. For the first time, it occurred to me that the sound really might be the wind after all. I had never felt anything quite like it. It appeared to have come out of nowhere, and it seemed like it was blowing in several directions at once. The trees were so bent over from it, they looked like they were about to snap. My hair blew up and whipped me in the face.

But then I heard the howling again, and I knew it couldn't be the wind. Something was out there. I leaned into the wind and took a few steps forward toward the woods.

Just then a huge gust blew right at me. At the same time, the lights in all the cabins went out.

It was completely dark, and the wind was

very strong. There was snow swirling all around me and the clouds were so thick that I couldn't see the moon — if there was one. But ahead of me, I could hear the howling, crying sound rising clearly above the sound of the wind.

I felt like I was being pulled toward it. It sounded so sad and full of pain that I felt almost like crying myself. I stumbled forward through the wind, toward the haunting sound.

After a few moments, my eyes began to adjust to the darkness. I squinted against the wind so I could see where I was.

Everywhere I looked there were trees, their branches waving wildly in the wind, creating strange shadows in the distance. Sometimes a branch would brush against me from behind, like a hand reaching out of the night. My heart was in my mouth.

I heard the sound again, but much louder this time. I knew I must be getting closer. The strong wind whipped the snow off the ground and into my face. I pulled my sleeping bag tighter around me. Suddenly, I saw something move out of the corner of my eye. Was it a shadow from the trees?

I turned my head. The thing moved again. It wasn't just a shadow. There was something huge and dark walking through the trees. And it was coming closer! Oh, how I wished I had listened to my grandmother! But it was too late. I had spent the night on Eagle Mountain, and now Eagle Feather was angry with me.

I stumbled backward against a tree, trying to hide myself in the branches. My heart was beating so loudly that I could hear it over the sounds of the wind and the horrible, longing moaning that kept coming closer and closer. My eyes were locked on the dark shadow that crouched in the trees in front of me. Suddenly, the moaning changed. It got louder and higher. The shadow was almost at my feet! I started to scream —

Chapter Ten

Two seconds later I was on my back in the snow, tangled up in my sleeping bag and eighty pounds of whimpering, licking dog. It was Alfie!

"Alfie! Down, Alfie! Good dog!" I called shakily. With one last lick of my face, Alfie backed off enough for me to sit up and untangle myself from my sleeping bag. My racing heart began to slow down, and I was able to think calmly about what had just happened. I had been so sure that I was going to meet the spirit of Eagle Feather out in the woods that I had completely ignored the fact that the wailing sounded just like a dog howling. I had to laugh at myself.

I stood up and looked for Alfie. He had moved a few feet away and was looking back at me. I started walking slowly toward him. It was too cold and windy for a dog to be out in the woods. I thought I should bring him back to the lodge.

"It's okay, Alfie, here I come," I said gently.

When I got to him, I reached out my hand to pat his head. I was going to try to lead him back by holding on to his collar. But before I could touch him, Alfie ran about ten feet ahead of me and stopped to look back again. I followed again, realizing that he was probably almost as scared as I had been.

As I drew closer, Alfie started walking again, staying just out of reach in front of me. I tried to keep up for a moment or two, then stopped. In the darkness, all I could see were trees. One direction looked the same as another, and I had no idea where I was.

"Alfie," I called over the wind. "Come here boy. . . please?" I walked forward again, more slowly. This time, Alfie stood still. I moved in beside him, grabbed his collar with one hand, and hugged him tight with the other. "Do you know where we are, Alfie?"

The wind suddenly doubled its force. The tree branches were lashing back and forth like live things. Snow was flying up from the ground and down from the tree branches and whirling around and around. It felt as if the entire mountain was angry.

Alfie started to whimper. I felt like crying myself. I was out in the woods in the middle of the night with no idea where I was. If someone came looking for me, I probably wouldn't be able to hear them over the wind or see them through the trees and swirling snow. I was really scared, but somehow I couldn't turn back.

I bent down and stroked Alfie's soft head. I couldn't get over how much he looked like a real wolf out here in the woods.

"It's okay," I said. "We'll keep each other company. Won't we, little wolf?"

Then I remembered. Little Wolf! That had been Eagle Feather's son's name. Maybe Running Deer's song would help me calm down. After all, it had worked when I was a baby, hadn't it?

I sat down on a tree stump and began to hum the lullaby. Right away I felt a little bit warmer and safer. It seemed to make Alfie feel better, too. He put his head down against my leg. His fur was so warm. I began to relax.

I started to sing the words to the lullaby out loud:

*"Otter, go to your home by the river, and Deer,
to lie in the woods.
Wolf, run back to your den, and Eagle, fly to
your perch."*

Then I noticed something strange. The wind seemed to be dying down. I sang louder.

*"Rabbit, crawl into your hole, and Serpent,
slide into your nest.
Wildcat, lay your head on your paws, and Bear,
crawl into your cave."*

The wind was almost completely gone.
*"Owl and Moon, watch over them all,
And Child close your eyes and sleep with the
world."*

The air was still, calm, and quiet, and Alfie lay sleeping on my leg. We were sitting in the middle of a small, hidden clearing. There wasn't a sound in the woods. I looked up at the trees. They had stopped moving.

Then I felt something wet on my nose. It was snowing! Tiny flakes of snow had begun drifting silently to the ground. I wondered if the crying sound hadn't been Alfie at all. Was it possible that there really was a ghost? My grandmother had said that the spirit of Eagle Feather would never rest until he felt Running Deer's spirit on the mountain again. And I had just been singing Running Deer's lullaby to soothe Alfie and myself when we were afraid. Could it be that the lullaby had really worked? Or was it just another coincidence? I didn't know what to think.

Then I saw a yellow beam of light a little way off between the trees. It seemed to be coming toward us. Alfie woke up and barked happily.

I heard someone call my name.

"Over here!" I yelled.

The light jiggled as it came closer, and soon I could make out a group of people. Katie was holding her flashlight, and she was accompanied by Randy, Sabs, Sam, Nick, Jason, Greg, B.Z., Laurel, Eva, and even Stacy!

Everything was all right again. I patted Alfie again and started walking toward my friends. I had hardly taken two steps when I felt something brush past my cheek. I turned quickly, just in time to see a feather drift to the ground. Holding my breath, I reached down and picked it up. It was an eagle feather, just like the one I had found in my school locker! I touched it carefully. It was all I needed to understand what had happened tonight. Eagle Feather was at peace. I slipped the feather into the inside pocket of my jacket for safekeeping.

"There you are!" said Randy.

"Allison, we were so worried!" said Sabrina.

"What were you doing all the way out here in the woods?" asked Stacy.

"Look, it's that dog!" said Nick.

"What's Alfie doing out here?" asked Sam.

I looked at them all. I didn't know where to begin.

"You must have been so scared," said Katie, putting her arm around my shoulders. "I mean it was so windy, and it's so dark out here. I bet you couldn't see anything. Especially after they shut the lights off for the night!"

So that's why all the lights went out, I thought. I had forgotten that the rangers turned the lights out at ten o'clock every night.

We walked back to the cabin, with Alfie frisking along behind us. I knew I had some explaining to do.

And I knew that I had to tell them the real story of the ghost of Eagle Mountain.

I just hoped they would understand.

Chapter Eleven

When we got inside, Randy took the flash-light from Katie, and attached it to the ceiling fixture. It filled the whole cabin with a warm glow.

"Come over here, Al," Katie said, leading me to one of the bunks when we got inside. Sabs wrapped my feet in one of her sweaters, and everyone gathered around me waiting for me to explain. Even Alfie came over and lay at my feet.

"I guess you're all wondering why I rushed outside?" I said, looking from one face to another.

"You can say that again," answered Nick.

"Yeah, I guess it was one of your ghostly ancestors, right?" asked Greg, with a silly smirk on his face.

"Shut up Loggins, or I'll deck ya" said Sam.

No one said anything else to Greg but Nick gave him a really mean look.

"Go on, Allison," said Sabrina.

I felt nervous. I guess I was afraid that they would think I was silly, or that they wouldn't be interested in the story after all. And I wasn't really used to talking about myself or my family in front of a lot of people. But then I remembered the ghost story that Ranger Rob had told earlier that night, and I knew that I wanted them to know my version, too.

I took a deep breath. "Well," I began, "first of all, that story that Ranger Rob told you isn't the only story. And it's not even the truth."

"That's obvious," said Greg. "It was just some dumb story he made up to scare us."

"Well, not exactly," I said, trying to ignore Greg's obnoxious tone. "It is true that a tribe of Native Americans used to live on this mountain. They were Chippewa. But the chief of the tribe was called Eagle Feather, not Flying Eagle. And he wasn't really wild and terrifying. At least, not when he was alive."

"What do you mean?" asked Eva.

"You mean this Eagle guy was a real person?" Greg asked. "No way!"

"Eagle Feather," Sabrina reminded him. "And if Allison says he was a real person, then he was a real person. Now be quiet and let her go on."

"Well," I continued. "Eagle Feather had a wife whose name was Running Deer, and they loved each other very much. They had a little baby named Little Wolf."

"Those are kind of funny names," Jason remarked.

"Not to a Chippewa. Native Americans often name their children after things they admire in nature. Nature is very important to them. Eagle Mountain was their home for many generations — before they were sent to the reservations, of course.

"Actually, that's sort of what the whole story is about. Nature and home — land, that is. You see, this whole area once belonged to Eagle Feather's tribe."

"Really?" said Eva.

"What happened?" asked Katie.

"Well, some settlers came, and they wanted the land. So there was a big battle, and Eagle Feather went off to fight. He left Running Deer and Little Wolf behind at home. The Chippewa lost the battle because the settlers had guns and they didn't."

"That doesn't sound very fair," said Laurel.

"No, it probably wasn't," I agreed. "Anyway, Eagle Feather managed to escape, but when he got back home, Running Deer and Little Wolf were gone."

"Where did they go?" asked Sabrina.

"Nobody knows," I answered. "But Eagle Feather supposedly searched the mountain for them for fifty-three days."

"Like in Ranger Rob's story!" said Nick excitedly.

"Yeah, but don't you see," I said, "it's not like in Ranger Rob's story at all. Eagle Feather wasn't wild and terrible. He was somebody's husband and somebody's father. He was off fighting to protect his land and his family."

"So what happened after the fifty-three days?" asked Randy.

"Well, they say he just disappeared," I said. "No one knows what happened to him. They think he probably died of loneliness. Or maybe from the cold. And that's why the Chippewa say that his spirit still roams this mountain."

"Oh," said Katie, "that's so sad."

"I can't believe that Ranger Rob guy messed up the story like that!" Nick exclaimed.

"You mean you guys really believe this?" Greg said. "Don't be such jerks."

Sabrina stood up. "Don't you be a jerk!" she said. "I believe every word of Allison's story! And if you don't, why don't you just go back to your own cabin where you belong!"

We all stared at her. I couldn't believe my ears.

"Fine," said Greg, standing up. "Who wants to hang around with a bunch of wimps anyway?"

He stamped across the floor, threw open the cabin door, and slammed it shut behind him. All that noise must have finally disturbed Miss Miller, because we could hear her roll over in her bed and begin to mumble to herself.

Katie glanced nervously at the door to her room. "You guys better go, too," she said, "or else we're all going to be in big trouble."

"Yeah, I guess you're right," said Sam. "Thanks for telling us about Eagle Feather, Allison."

"Yeah," said Nick. "Sorry Greg was such a jerk."

"Bye. See you tomorrow," said Jason as

they shut the door behind them.

"Nice going, Sabs," said Randy. "You really told Greg."

Laurel agreed. "To think I used to think he was kind of cute."

Sabrina looked at her. "You too?" she asked.

"Sure," said Laurel, "but not anymore. I mean, he's still good-looking, but he's not nice at all."

"Allison, you still haven't told us why you ran out in the woods like that, and where Alfie came from," Katie reminded me.

"Well, it's sort of hard to explain," I said. "But ever since I first heard about this ski trip, I had bad feelings about it. It started the day our names were posted on the bulletin board. I went to my locker right after that, and a beautiful eagle feather floated right out of my locker onto the floor. It bothered me because my grandfather collects eagle feathers, so I know what they look like and how rare they are."

"Yeah!" said Randy excitedly. "I remember you telling me something about feathers, the night before we came up here!"

Sabrina's eyes opened wide. "I bet it's

Eagle Feather trying to give you a sign!" she said excitedly.

"That's what I'm beginning to think," I said smiling at her. "Anyway, that night my grandmother told me the story of Eagle Feather and I felt even worse. You see, the Chippewa believe it is wrong to come up on the mountain and sleep here, because it disturbs the spirit of Eagle Feather."

"Really?" asked Sabrina, widening her eyes.

"Yes," I told her. "And then when the bus broke down, and we got lost on the trail, I kept wondering if there could be any truth to the old superstition. So when we heard that crying sound outside, I just had to find out what it was. I had to know if it really was Eagle Feather."

"Well, was it?" asked Laurel.

"Yeah, did you see anything?" Randy wanted to know.

"It's kind of hard to say. First of all, there was that incredible wind. And I definitely heard some kind of wailing out there. It could have been Alfie. After all, I found him out in the woods — or he found me." I smiled and scratched Alfie's ears again.

"And there's another thing. In the story, there's this song that Running Deer used to sing when she put Little Wolf to sleep at night."

"You mean like 'Rock-a-bye Baby' or something?" asked Randy.

"Well, sort of, but not exactly. It's about all of the animals in the woods going to sleep for the night. Supposedly, the last time Eagle Feather saw Running Deer, she was singing it to the baby. And they say that his spirit can't rest until he feels her spirit again. I thought it might have something to do with the song."

"Do you know it?" asked Katie.

"Yeah, when I was out there in the woods and I got scared because I couldn't see the cabin since the lights were out, I started to sing it to myself so I would calm down. And then a funny thing happened."

Sabrina leaned forward. "What? Did you see Eagle Feather?" she asked.

"No, not exactly," I told her. "The thing was, once I started singing, it didn't only calm me down, but everything else seemed to calm down, too. The wind stopped. Alfie relaxed so much that he fell asleep. And then it started to snow."

"Hey, that must have been just about the time we set out to look for you," Katie said. "I remember stepping outside the cabin and seeing snowflakes in the beam of my flashlight!"

"I remember, too," said Sabs.

"And then when Allison sang the song out in the woods, everything calmed down," said Katie.

"But wait! You haven't heard the most amazing thing of all," I said, leaning closer to them.

"What?" asked Sabrina.

"Well, the moment you guys found me another feather appeared as we were walking away. Here it is!" I said excitedly, holding the feather up to show them.

"Totally cool," Randy said thoughtfully. "Allison sang a lullaby to a ghost!"

"And it worked!" said Katie.

"How did you know what song to sing?" Eva asked.

"My grandmother taught it to me," I said. "She used to sing it to put me to sleep when I was a baby. It's really pretty. At least, I think so."

"Oh, Allison, sing it to us!" said Sabrina.

"Allison," said Stacy, "I've never heard a Chippewa lullaby, I'd love to hear it."

"Oh, yes, please!" said Katie.

"I want to hear it, too," said Randy. "This has to be some lullaby if it put the whole mountain to sleep!"

I hesitated for a minute. But they all looked so interested that I felt like I couldn't really say no.So I opened my mouth and began to sing the song, quietly at first, and then a little louder. First I sang just the Chippewa words, then I added the english words that my mother had taught me:

"Otter, go to your home by the river, and Deer,
to lie in the woods.
Wolf, run back to your den, and Eagle, fly to
your perch.
Rabbit, crawl into your hole, and Serpent, slide
into your nest.
Wildcat, lay your head on your paws, and Bear,
crawl into your cave.
Owl and Moon, watch over them all,
And Child, close your eyes and sleep with the

world.

Sabrina sighed when I finished. "Oh, Allison, that was beautiful."

"Sing it again, so we can learn it," Katie begged.

I sang the song a couple more times, and by the third time, everyone was singing along.

Suddenly, the door to the other room opened, and Miss Miller stood there with a furious look on her face.

She was wearing a big yellow-plaid nightgown, and her hair was in curlers. There was some kind of cream all over her face.

"Don't you think it's awfully late to be up singing?" she asked angrily. I knew I couldn't look at anyone else or I would burst out laughing.

"I expect you all to be sound asleep within five minutes!" she went on. "Remember, we want to be out on the trails bright and early tomorrow morning." She turned and went back into her room, banging the door behind her.

We looked at each other and started laughing. We tried very hard to keep quiet so Miss

Miller wouldn't hear us again, but that just made us laugh harder.

I wiped my eyes. "I can't believe she slept through all that stuff — the boys, and the wind, and the howling — and finally it was a lullaby that woke her up," I said.

"It's a good thing she didn't notice Alfie," said Katie.

"Really," said Randy. "She might have scared him in that getup."

We climbed into our sleeping bags.

"Oh, no," said Katie. "We forgot to turn off the flashlight."

"Maybe we should just sleep with it on," said Laurel.

. "I'll turn it off," I said. Somehow I knew there wasn't anything to be afraid of anymore.

Suddenly Sabs spoke to me in the darkness.

"Allison," she said, "what do you think? Do you believe the story? Do you think Eagle Feather's ghost roams Eagle Mountain?"

I thought for a moment. "I don't know," I answered. "Some strange things happened here tonight. And it's definitely true that the lullaby is a powerful song. When I was out there in the woods, it really made me feel a lot better."

"Wow, Al, this story is really cool," said Randy.

"You're so lucky," said Eva. "I wish I knew more about my family and their past."

"I know what you mean," said Katie. "I wish my grandmother would tell me stuff like that."

I felt Alfie climb up onto my bunk and settle himself down around my feet. I smiled to myself. I hadn't ever thought of myself as lucky in quite that way before. I loved my family, especially my grandmother with her old-fashioned ways. But I had never realized how lucky I was to have her stories, too. She made me proud to be a Chippewa, proud of my heritage. Smiling, I hummed the lullaby until I fell into a very peaceful sleep.

Titles in the GIRL TALK series

1 WELCOME TO JUNIOR HIGH!
Introducing the Girl Talk characters, Sabrina Wells, Katie Campbell, Randy Zak, and Allison Cloud. When our four heroines meet and have to plan the first junior high dance of the year, the results are hilarious.

2 FACE-OFF!
Katie Campbell is just plain fed up with being "perfect." But when she decides to join the boys' ice hockey team, she gets more than she bargained for.

3 THE NEW YOU
Allison Cloud's world turns upside down when she is chosen to model for *Belle* magazine with Stacy the Great!

4 REBEL, REBEL
Randy Zak is acting even stranger than usual. Could a visit from her cute New York friend have something to do with it?

5 IT'S ALL IN THE STARS
Sabrina gets even when she discovers that someone is playing a practical joke on her — and all her horoscopes are coming true.

6 THE GHOST OF EAGLE MOUNTAIN
The girls go on a weekend ski trip, only to discover that they're sleeping on the very spot where the Ghost of Eagle Mountain wanders!

LOOK FOR THE GIRL TALK BOOKS!
COMING SOON TO A BOOKSTORE NEAR YOU!

LOOK FOR THESE GIRL TALK GAMES AND PRODUCTS!

Girl Talk Games:
- Girl Talk Game
- Girl Talk Second Edition
- Girl Talk Travel Game
- Girl Talk Date Line

Girl Talk Puzzles:
- Hunk
- Heart to Heart

The Girl Talk Collection:
- Blushers
- Lip Gloss
- Hair Fashions
- 20 Anywhere Stickers
- Slumber Party Kit
- Eye Shadow
- Fingernails
- Paints that Puff
- Fantasy Fortune Party Kit

TALK BACK!

TELL US WHAT YOU THINK ABOUT GIRL TALK

Name _Regina Healy_

Address _4408 83rd Ave N._

City _Brooklyn Park_ State _MN_ Zip _55443_

Birthday: Day _10_ Mo _Sept_ Year _81_

Telephone Number (_612_) _560-0869_

1) On a scale of 1 (The Pits) to 5 (The Max),
how would you rate Girl Talk?   Circle One:

1   2   ③   4   5

2) What do you like most about Girl Talk?

___Characters _✓_Situations___Telephone Talk

Other _____

3) Who is your favorite character?   Circle One:

Sabrina   (Katie)   Randy

Allison   Stacy   Other

4) Who is your least favorite character?

Stacey sometimes

5) What do you want to read about in Girl Talk?

Situations and
everything else

Send completed form to :
Western Publishing Company, Inc.
1220 Mound Avenue Mail Station #85
Racine, Wisconsin 53404